C O F F E E   W I T H

HEMINGWAY

KIRK CURNUTT

FOREWORD BY JOHN UPDIKE

DUNCAN BAIRD PUBLISHERS

LONDON

Coffee with Hemingway
Kirk Curnutt

Distributed in the USA and Canada by
Sterling Publishing Co., Inc.
387 Park Avenue South
New York, NY 10016-8810

This edition first published in the UK and USA in 2007 by
Duncan Baird Publishers Ltd
Sixth Floor, Castle House
75–76 Wells Street, London W1T 3QH

Managing Editors: Peggy Vance and Gill Paul
Co-ordinating Editors: Daphne Razazan and James Hodgson
Editor: Kirsty Seymour-Ure
Assistant Editor: Kirty Topiwala
Managing Designer: Clare Thorpe

Library of Congress Cataloging-in-Publication Data Available
ISBN-10: 1-84483-514-6   ISBN-13: 978-1-84483-514-0
10 9 8 7 6 5 4 3 2 1
Printed in China

For information about custom editions, special sales, premium and corporate
purchases, please contact Sterling Special Sales Department at 800-805-5489
or specialsales@sterlingpub.com.

Publisher's note:
The interviews in this book are purely fictional, while having a solid basis in
biographical fact. They take place between a fictionalized Ernest Hemingway
and an imaginary interviewer.

CONTENTS

Foreword by JOHN UPDIKE

In the near half-century since Hemingway's shocking suicide by shotgun in 1961, his fame—and did any American writer of the 20th century enjoy more fame than he?—has attracted denigration, from critics and academics who react, perhaps, more to the man's image than his works. He whose hero, in *A Farewell to Arms*, is a deserter from World War I, and whose portrait of civil war in *For Whom the Bell Tolls* unsparingly reports the atrocities on both sides, is accused of being a lover of violence. His boyhood as a Midwestern doctor's son and his war wounds in Italy at the age of eighteen impressed him with the reality of violence, and his fiction and nonfiction (see *Death in the Afternoon* and his introduction to his anthology *Men at War*) sought to describe this reality, including the hunter's blood lust; but a fascination is not an endorsement. He is accused of slighting his female characters, yet they—Brett and Catherine and Maria—dominate the canvases of their respective novels, and remain more poignantly, sympathetically, and heroically in the mind than their male lovers do.

Hemingway's apparently simple style, easily parodied, is dismissed as semi-literate when in fact it was a refined and thoughtful product of modernism in its youthful prime; he took English prose and, in Ezra Pound's phrase, made it new. The example of modern painting, above all the scrupulous post-impressionism of Cézanne, inspired him; newspaper work honed his powers of distillation; wide reading kept his standards elevated. To be sure, he liked a fiesta, and drank too much, but he reported to his writing stand, with freshly sharpened pencils, each dawn; his writing forms a shimmering paean to our physical existence, to landscape and weather and healthy senses. His stoic hedonism became, in the ruin of conventional pieties left by World War I, a creed for his generation, a laconic lifestyle reflected in popular films, other people's writing, and even common speech.

His first book, published in 1923 in Paris, was titled *Three Stories and Ten Poems*; his short stories, which he effectively stopped producing after collecting them in 1938, are like poems in their concision, polish, and enigmatic abruptness. A sense of life's tragic brevity always lies beneath the surfaces of his taut dialogues and evocations of nature. Only the first two novels, *The Sun Also Rises* (1926) and *A Farewell to Arms* (1929), sustain throughout their length the exquisite economy and freshness of the short stories, though the novella *The Old Man and the Sea* (1952) approached their high quality and helped win the author the Nobel

Prize in 1954. In his later years, in shaky physical and mental health, he published almost nothing but wrote steadily, accumulating masses of manuscripts that were mined for a number of posthumous publications, of which the most valuable is a fond memoir of his Paris years, *A Moveable Feast* (1964).

The man was a bearish celebrity when literature still bred celebrities; his work remains a touchstone of artistic ardor and luminously clean prose.

John Updike

INTRODUCTION

Nearly 50 years after his death, Ernest Hemingway remains arguably the most famous and influential American writer ever. His prominence has not wavered since 1926, when *The Sun Also Rises* made him a symbol of living gracefully amid the upheaval of the post-World War I era. Hemingway continues to inspire because, on the surface at least, he promises us that the line between life's twin compulsions—to work and to play—can be seamless if only we approach every experience with the ethical rigor and exactitude of ritual. Whatever act we might undertake—eating, fishing, loving, boxing, writing—he assures us that there is a right way to do it, and that we can intuit that way if we cleanse the moral palate and keep our poise.

With icon status comes oversimplification, however, and the spell Hemingway casts has ensured that his qualities will be distorted to the point of caricature. For every enthusiast who has tried to write in a Montparnasse café (I'm guilty of this), fish the Gulf Stream (ditto), or run with the bulls in Pamplona (alas, I lack the necessary *cojones*), there's a resisting reader for whom Hemingway can never connote anything but cartoon machismo and misogyny and an overheated stoicism and existential angst. Yet for all the posturing, Hemingway had a keen capacity for knowing when he had dropped the purity of his own line, and he would castigate himself with the same ferocity to which he subjected his rivals during his celebrated literary squabbles.

Because the complexities of Hemingway's personality are frequently overlooked, I often find myself imagining interviewing him with the express aim of drawing out his nuances: the self-excoriation of "The Snows of Kilimanjaro," the remorseful nostalgia of *A Moveable Feast*, the wounded idealism of *In Our Time*, and the pragmatic heroism of *For Whom the Bell Tolls*. That's not to leave out the playful pontifications that irked critics of *Death in the Afternoon*, or the often over-the-top muscularity of *To Have and Have Not*, or even the Rabelaisian bawdiness of his correspondence. In trying to capture these contradictory voices, the imaginary conversation that follows aspires to return dimensionality to a man whom popular culture has shrouded in truisms and clichés. It also grants him an opportunity to defend himself against modern-day misperceptions. Most of all, this book aims to emphasize the qualities that made him a great writer. With an eye for *le bon mot*, an ear for rhythm, and a talent for saying more with less, Hemingway invigorated literature with an urgency and subtle poignancy that remains as moving in our time as it was in his.

ERNEST HEMINGWAY (1899–1961)
His Life in Short

"He wanted to be a great writer," Hemingway says
of his alter ego Nick Adams during a contemplative
moment in the original draft of "Big Two-Hearted
River," the classic 1924 story of a fishing expedition
in upper Michigan. "He was pretty sure he would be.
He knew it in lots of ways." Although the nine-page
meditation in which this admission of ambition
appears was eventually deleted, the passage remains
intriguing, for it offers an unguarded glimpse of the
confidence that convinced the young doctor's son
from Oak Park, Illinois, that he was destined for
literary eminence. When Hemingway wrote these
words, his collected works encompassed only a
smattering of sketches and short stories published in
obscure avant-garde journals and two small, privately

printed booklets. By contrast, F. Scott Fitzgerald's debut novel, *This Side of Paradise*, had sold nearly 50,000 copies in 1920, its first year of publication, and his tales of flappers and their starry-eyed beaus were earning outrageous sums from high-circulation slicks such as the *Saturday Evening Post*.

Yet barely a year after finishing "Big Two-Hearted River," Hemingway would be hailed as the most original voice of his generation. In addition to "River," several stories in an expanded version of *In Our Time* (1925) proved revolutionary for depicting 20th-century brutality in frank and uncompromising language. The following year *The Sun Also Rises* made him a youth-culture spokesman by inspiring post-collegians galore to repair to expatriate Paris and Pamplona. By the time of his second story collection, *Men Without Women* (1927)—featuring the oft-anthologized "The Killers" and "Hills Like White

Elephants"—he was recognized as the originator of a brittle literary minimalism built upon hardboiled bursts of dialogue. Barely 30 when *A Farewell to Arms* was published in 1929, Hemingway was no longer merely an artist but a celebrity, an avatar of adventuresome vitality and sporty manhood. So infectious was his style that other writers had to strive not to sound like him. His popular audience, meanwhile, lived vicariously through what the press trumpeted as his glamorous globetrotting.

One thing often overlooked within the larger outline of Hemingway's biography is the importance of his work ethic. "First there must be talent," he argues in *Green Hills of Africa* (1935). "Then there must be discipline … Then there must be the conception of what it can be and an absolute conscience as unchanging as the standard meter in Paris, to prevent faking."

This "absolute conscience" was largely the legacy of his father, Clarence Edmonds Hemingway (1871–1928), a respected though not prominent general practitioner whose gruff and stolid reputation reflected his abhorrence of loafing. Even at the family's summer home on Walloon Lake near Petoskey, Michigan, the father insisted that his six children adopt a devoutly ethical approach to recreation. The hunting, camping, and fishing that Ernest grew up learning were not diversions but self-improving moral exercises. Clarence's Victorian belief in self-regulation and self-improvement imbued Hemingway with a seriousness of purpose that would reverberate in his descriptions of even the simplest of leisure activities. The stern professionalism of his ethos likewise reflects Clarence's rectitude. The disparaging judgments that he would level against his peers echo the admonitions against indolence that he grew up hearing from his father.

The other pronounced aspect of Hemingway's personality, his penchant for showmanship, was inherited from his mother, Grace Hall Hemingway (1872–1951), an amateur contralto and painter. Although Hemingway came to loathe his mother— blaming her overbearingness for the harrowing depressions that Clarence suffered—his charisma and restless enthusiasm came from her. Later biographers such as Kenneth Lynn have depicted Grace as emasculating Ernest, first by dressing him and his older sister, Marcelline (1898–1963), as androgynous identical twins in their childhood, and later by inveigling him into a "deliciously intimate dependency" by disapproving of the very unapologetic individuality she had bequeathed him. Yet Mrs. Hemingway was hardly an overbearing or domineering mother. She was, rather, like many artists, a little self-preoccupied—a trait her son would also absorb. As with many Victorian-bred parents, she was also ill-prepared to deal with the generation gap separating her from her modern-minded son, an inability that sometimes rendered her incapable of appreciating his literary accomplishments—in 1951 she told a Detroit newspaper that she considered Ernest's schoolboy essays to be better than his books. For all the praise he received throughout his career, Hemingway could never quite overcome such disapproval. "She hates my guts," he complained around the time of that interview, which infuriated him so much he threatened to cut off financial support.

However much Hemingway's personality was shaped by his oddly paired parents, his writing could not have developed as it did had he not left the conservative environs of Oak Park after graduating from high school in 1917. A series of formative experiences began to shape his sensibility. Eschewing college, he worked as a cub reporter for the *Kansas City Star*, whose style sheet offered "the best rules I ever learned for the business of writing." Later collected as *Ernest Hemingway: Cub Reporter* (1970), the dozen or so unsigned pieces produced during his tenure reveal the influence of *Star* dos and don'ts, such as "Use short sentences" and "Avoid the use of adjectives." They also introduce his fascination with the seamy underside of crime, whose gangsters and gunmen would reappear in "The Killers" and his most noirish novel, *To Have and Have Not* (1937).

Even more decisive was Hemingway's service as an ambulance driver for the American Red Cross in Italy in mid-1918. Like many young men his age, Ernest was eager to see combat after the United

States entered the Great War in November 1917. He had grown up hearing stories of both of his grandfathers' exploits during the American Civil War and imagined himself carrying on their heroism. Yet poor eyesight prevented him from enlisting, and he went abroad as a relief worker rather than a soldier. Less than a month into his service, on July 8, 1918, he was seriously wounded in a mortar attack along the Piave River near the city of Fossalta, his legs and groin riddled with shrapnel. The wounding became the formative event of his career. Both his terror and the heroism credited to him (he was awarded an Italian medal of valor for tending to Italian soldiers caught in the same attack) form the central motifs of *In Our Time*, *A Farewell to Arms*, and several stories.

His subsequent recuperation at the Red Cross Hospital in Milan introduced him to a second integral theme. While there he fell in love with an

American nurse, Agnes von Kurowsky (1892–1984).
Yet two months after he returned to Oak Park in
January 1919 she informed him that their courtship
was over, even though Ernest was telling his friends
that they were engaged. Love and war were thus
inexorably mingled in Hemingway's mind, with
both *A Farewell to Arms* and *For Whom the Bell Tolls*
(1940) bitterly insisting that, in a world rife with
the latter, the former cannot provide any escape
from pain.

The third formative experience didn't occur until
December 1921, when Hemingway expatriated to
Paris at the suggestion of author Sherwood Anderson
(1876–1941) to join the burgeoning modern arts
movement. By that time he was newly married to
Hadley Richardson (1891–1979), whom he'd met
in Chicago while freelancing for the *Toronto Daily
Star*. Despite Hemingway's war experience, early

attempts at fictionalizing it were no more than pale imitations of the Rudyard Kipling adventures he'd read as a boy. As Anderson promised, the American colony in Paris was revolutionizing literature, inventing new methods for conveying the uncertain temper of the times. Accordingly, once in Paris, the Hemingways ingratiated themselves with modernist luminaries such as Gertrude Stein (1873–1946) and Ezra Pound (1885–1972). Absorbing the heady atmosphere that was producing such landmarks as James Joyce's *Ulysses* (1922), Hemingway quickly found his voice through painstaking writing exercises he developed for himself, despite the necessity of posting stories for the *Star*, for which he served as a foreign correspondent through 1923. Hemingway learned from Stein how to vary his sentences through rhythm and repetition. He also assimilated her ideas on description, a subject she lectured on while showing off her impressive collection of paintings by Paul Cézanne, Henri Matisse, and Pablo Picasso. And while Pound introduced him to experimental techniques that pared his sentences down to imagistic fragments, his main influence was as a patron: it was thanks to Pound that 300 copies of *Three Stories and Ten Poems* were printed in 1923, officially inaugurating Hemingway's literary career.

That same year, at the invitation of the avant-garde journal *Little Review*, the author produced a sextet of violent vignettes involving war and bullfighting (to which Stein had introduced him). Viscerally immediate, the pieces were so sparsely worded that Hemingway called his technique "unwriting." Along with a subsequent dozen fragments, these "postcards from hell," as one critic describes them, formed the basis of *in our time*, a 170-copy collection published by friend and

fellow journalist William Bird's Three Mountains
Press. The small volume won Hemingway his first
critical acclaim, with Edmund Wilson (1895–1972)
proclaiming, "I am inclined to think that this little
book has more artistic dignity than any other that
has been written by an American about the period
of the war."

The year 1924 was to be Hemingway's *annus
mirabilis*, seeing the writing and/or publication of
several influential stories that defined his major
themes: the quest to establish one's place in nature
("Big Two-Hearted River"); initiation into a
knowledge of death and violence ("Indian Camp");
the war generation's estrangement from Victorian
values ("Soldier's Home"); and alienation and the
impermanence of love ("Out of Season" and "Cat in
the Rain," both of which equate marital instability
with expatriate isolation). Hemingway's aptitude for

networking and attracting publicity likewise elevated his reputation. By the time a commercial version of *in our time* appeared in 1925 from the New York publisher Boni & Liveright (its title now capitalized), many peers and aspiring writers were seeking him out as he previously had Stein and Pound.

In April 1925, he accidentally encountered F. Scott Fitzgerald (1896–1940) in the Dingo Bar, Paris, two weeks after the publication of *The Great Gatsby*. Fitzgerald would be instrumental in finessing his friend's relationship with editor Maxwell Perkins at Charles Scribner's Sons, which would become Hemingway's exclusive publisher starting with the satire *The Torrents of Spring* (1926).

Six weeks after meeting Fitzgerald, Ernest and Hadley departed for Hemingway's third trip to the San Fermín bullfighting festival in Pamplona, Spain. Thanks to a rowdy entourage of fellow expatriates, the trip was muddled with sexual jealousy and drunken fistfights, most inspired by a dissolute divorcée named Duff Twysden (1893–1938). Both intrigued and repulsed by Duff's disaffected lifestyle, Hemingway shortly transformed the trip into a roman-à-clef-cum-generational fable about postwar disillusionment. Originally entitled "The Lost Generation" (a phrase borrowed from Stein), *The Sun Also Rises* became a youth-cult phenomenon. Journalist Jake Barnes's inability to love the promiscuous Brett Ashley because of a debilitating war injury that renders him impotent symbolized his generation's belief that it lacked the ability to engage fully with life. Thanks in no small part to *The Sun*'s reputation as a guidebook to expatriate Paris, the novel became a *succès de scandale*, and Hemingway quickly supplanted Fitzgerald as the reigning spokesman for the under-30 set.

In contrast to this success, Hemingway's private life was in turmoil. In late 1926 he left Hadley and their son, John or "Bumby" (b. 1923), for Pauline Pfeiffer (1895–1951), a Paris *Vogue* staffer who'd recently joined the Hemingways' expatriate circle. Later, in *A Moveable Feast*, Hemingway would equate the end of his first marriage with the loss of his artistic purity. At the time, however, he was drawn to Pauline, the daughter of a prosperous entrepreneur from Piggott, Arkansas, because she was both worldlier and wealthier than the shy, sheltered Hadley. Ernest and Pauline married in April 1927 and returned to the United States in 1928, settling in Key West, Florida, which would become their base for the next decade. Drawing upon his war experience, Hemingway was by then into a second novel about another American wounded by war, this time a lieutenant in the Italian army, who falls in love with his Red Cross nurse. Work was interrupted in late 1928 by an event that would haunt his future fiction: on December 6, Clarence Hemingway killed himself with the same .32 caliber pistol that Ernest's revered grandfather, Anson, had carried during the Civil War. For three decades to come, Hemingway would grapple with the specter of his father's death, fending off his own "black ass" depressions while trying to decide whether suicide was heroic or cowardly.

Upon publication in September 1929, *A Farewell to Arms* was hailed as the quintessential World War I novel, thanks to Hemingway's gripping depiction of the Italian army's 1917 retreat from Caporetto, where they were routed by Austrian troops. "I was always embarrassed by the words sacred, glorious, and sacrifice," thinks Frederic Henry the night before the disastrous battle. "I had seen nothing sacred, and the things that were glorious had no glory and

the sacrifices were like the stockyards at Chicago
if nothing was done with the meat except to bury it."

A grim if sometimes melodramatic tragedy, in
which Lieutenant Henry deserts the war to retrieve
Catherine Barkley, only to lose her and their stillborn
child to a botched Caesarean section, *Farewell*
introduced Hemingway to a much wider popular
audience than *In Our Time* or even *The Sun*—selling
nearly 30,000 copies in its first month despite
the near-simultaneous onslaught of the Great
Depression. The novel also cemented his reputation
as a consummate craftsman. Thanks to a breathless
New Yorker profile by Dorothy Parker (1893–1967),
Hemingway became known for the dedicated hard
work and sheer graft that he put into his art. As
"proof," Parker told the story of how Hemingway
rewrote the ending of *Farewell* 70 times—which was
only a slight exaggeration (it was actually 28 times).

Despite *Farewell*'s success—or perhaps because of it—almost a decade would pass before Hemingway completed another book-length fiction. Instead, the 1930s marked the emergence of his "Papa" persona, the querulous, often hectoring grand master of American letters who might produce a short-story classic such as "A Clean, Well-Lighted Place" (1933) when not trawling the Gulf of Mexico in his custom fishing boat, the *Pilar*, hunting kudu on the Serengeti, or posing for magazine photos with his boys (a third son, Gregory, was born in 1931). Yet popular misperceptions of this era do a severe disservice to the nonfiction to which the author now devoted his attention. While reviewers panned both *Death in the Afternoon* (1932) and *Green Hills of Africa* (1935), these books are nevertheless fascinating for their mixture of styles, voices, and genres—all tightly regulated by a ritualistic regard for the morality

of sport. The former finds Hemingway drawing
constant parallels between bullfighting and writing
as he defines artistic standards of authenticity.
The latter, a record of Ernest and Pauline's 1933–34
African safari, offers some of his richest descriptions
of landscape. In between these efforts, Hemingway
became a regular contributor to *Esquire*, a new men's
magazine that mingled fashion and fiction. His
dispatches from Cuba, Key West, and Africa provide
insight into the author's politics, his notions of
masculinity, and his irritation at his own celebrity.

   This period marked a severe reassessment of
his literary merits. When his story collection *Winner
Take Nothing* appeared in 1933, reviewers complained
that such efforts as "Wine of Wyoming" and "The
Gambler, the Nun, and the Radio" suggested "a lack
of growth" and a "monotonous repetition of subjects
... eating and drinking, travel, sport, coition."

Unfortunately, *To Have and Have Not*, Hemingway's first novel since *A Farewell to Arms*, did little to reverse this opinion. In drafting the novel, the author even referenced his own decline, with one character bicycling past the Hemingways' home at 907 Whitehead Street to note how the "big slob" living there had failed his promise. Although Hemingway deleted this scene from his final version, he did allow one stunning example of self-repudiation into print. In his greatest short story, "The Snows of Kilimanjaro" (1936), a writer dying from gangrene while on safari in Africa must admit to having squandered his talent through drinking and womanizing. All the memories Harry Walden has failed to transform into fiction come back to haunt him in the form of lyrical interior monologues that convey Hemingway's remorseful nostalgia for the heyday of 1920s Paris. Although the story takes rather

ungenerous swipes at Pauline and Fitzgerald,
there's no doubt that Hemingway is the real target
of his own irate disappointment.

Despite "Snows," the inspiration for
Hemingway's artistic renaissance was not his
personal regrets but the international scene. In
1937, he traveled to Spain to cover the civil war that
erupted when totalitarian troops under aspiring
dictator Francisco Franco attempted to unseat the
country's fledgling Republican government. Devoutly
anti-fascist, Hemingway lent his credibility and
celebrity to the leftist cause, helping to produce a
propagandistic documentary, *The Spanish Earth*,
while working as a correspondent for the North
American News Alliance. After four separate tours
of Spain in 1937–38, Hemingway realized that the
cause was doomed, and he retreated to Key West to
weigh the value of political commitment in a world

of corrupted ideologies. The result was *For Whom the Bell Tolls*, which, despite some stilted stream-of-consciousness interludes, many still regard as Hemingway's greatest novel. As with *A Farewell to Arms*, an impossible love story unfolds across the backdrop of war, with the American munitions expert Robert Jordan seeking to save a brutalized woman, Maria. Populated with colorful characters, *For Whom* echoed the message of *In Our Time* by insisting that the separate peace of personal integrity is the only reliable measure of morality when the fog of war makes heroes and villains indistinguishable. Thanks to its timeliness (the book appeared at the onset of World War II), it became Hemingway's greatest success yet, selling nearly 500,000 copies within its first six months.

As during the publication of *A Farewell to Arms*, Hemingway's private life was in turmoil, and yet another decade would pass before he again completed a book, much less a novel. In December 1936, he met the writer Martha Gellhorn (1908–1998), and their affair during the Spanish Civil War spelled the end for his second marriage. Ernest and Pauline were divorced in late 1940, by which point Hemingway and Gellhorn were living together at a Cuban estate called La Finca Vigía, making annual expeditions to Sun Valley, Idaho. Hemingway's third marriage was his shortest and unhappiest. Unaccustomed to a wife as devoted to her career as he was to his, he resented Martha's frequent absences on journalism assignments.

After the Japanese attack on Pearl Harbor in December 1941, Hemingway sought to assist in the war effort by patrolling the Gulf for German submarines. In 1944, eager to see the European front, he finagled press credentials from *Collier's* magazine (for which Gellhorn also worked) and covered the Allied landing on D-Day, before accompanying the Royal Air Force on bombing missions. He participated in the liberation of Paris and the Hürtgenwald Forest drive into Germany, eventually being called before the Army Inspector General for acting as a combatant rather than a correspondent.

In London, shortly before D-Day, Hemingway met journalist Mary Welsh (1908–1986), with whom he entered yet another extramarital relationship. Divorce from Gellhorn ensued, and the couple married in 1946, settling at the Finca Vigía, where Hemingway began a pair of projects that would not be read publicly until after his death: *Islands in the Stream* (1970) and *The Garden of Eden* (1986). When a new novel called *Across the River and Into the Trees* did finally appear in 1950, its May–December romance plot (based on the author's flirtation with an Italian teenager named Adriana Ivancich) was widely panned. Two years later, Hemingway rebounded with *The Old Man and the Sea*, a deceptively simple man-versus-nature story in which a poor Cuban fisherman, Santiago, loses a 1,000-pound (450 kg) marlin to marauding sharks. The book led to Hemingway's winning two prizes he had long coveted: the Pulitzer in 1953 and the Nobel in 1954.

Unlike most recipients of literature's most prestigious honor, Hemingway did not travel to Stockholm to address the Swedish Academy. His health was too poor. Only in his mid-fifties, he looked two decades older, thanks to alcoholism, hypertension, and the ravages of not one but two plane crashes survived on two consecutive days in Africa. Besieged by reporters, he spent much of 1954–55 trying to avoid publicity hounds in order to work on a semi-fictional account of the African safari that had occasioned the crashes. After years of being encouraged to write his autobiography, he started recording memories of expatriate Paris in 1956. Posthumously published as *A Moveable Feast* (1964), the sketches find Hemingway once again preaching his credo of disciplined artistry while offering unflattering vignettes of Stein, Fitzgerald, and other writers who failed his standards. Yet he saves his harshest judgments for himself, obliquely regretting the loss of his first wife and his corruption at the hands of flattering friends.

Hemingway had envisioned publishing his memoirs in 1960, followed by an update of *Death in the Afternoon* that would include an account of the spectacular 1959 bullfighting season. However, poor health, depression, and paranoia intervened. The Castro revolution forced Ernest and Mary from the Finca Vigía, and Hemingway grew convinced that the FBI was monitoring his activities—a concern that has since been substantiated. J. Edgar Hoover was indeed informed when, at Mary's insistence, Hemingway entered the Mayo Clinic in late 1960. (Hoover's interest was likely spurred by pro-Castro statements Hemingway made.) The electro-shock therapy received there exacerbated Ernest's condition, obliterating his memory and rendering him incapable of writing. Nevertheless, after two suicide attempts in April 1961, he returned to the clinic for additional treatments. Convincing his doctors he was cured, he was released in late June and returned to Ketchum, Idaho, where he and Mary owned a home.

There, on the morning of July 2, only two days after his arrival, he killed himself with his favorite 12-gauge Boss shotgun.

"I want to run as a writer," Hemingway wrote in a 1950 letter. "Not as a man who had been to wars; nor a bar room fighter; nor a shooter; nor a horse-player; nor a drinker. I would like to be a straight writer and be judged as such … " Since his death, admirers have not always honored this request. On any given day you can find them in Paris, Pamplona, Oak Park, Petoskey, Key West, Ketchum, and many other places searching for traces of the personality that saturates his every sentence. What was Hemingway *really* like? they want to know. The fact that new biographies, memoirs, and academic studies continue to appear year after year suggests just how elusive the answer finally is.

NOW LET'S START TALKING ...

Over the following pages, Ernest Hemingway
engages in an imaginary conversation (set in his
favorite Parisian café, the Closerie des Lilas), in
which he responds freely to searching questions.
The conversation covers ten themes.

The questions are in blue italic type;
Hemingway's answers are in brown type.

ERNIE AGONISTES

Hemingway no sooner achieved a measure of
renown than his personality changed: gone was
the sensitive aspiring writer known variously as
Hem, Wemedge, and Tatie, to be replaced by a
belligerent figure who lashed out at critics and
impetuously broke with friends. As Gertrude
Stein said, Hemingway seemed at war with
himself, his burly truculence becoming "a
disguise for the thing that was really gentle and
fine in him." As a result, discerning readers
have sought to understand why a writer so
capable of capturing emotional nuance allowed
himself, in the words of Edmund Wilson, to
become "his own worst-drawn character."

Sorry, I don't mean to interrupt while you're working,
but I need some advice. I have a war story I want to
write. I was hoping you might help me. Nobody writes
a better war story than you.

You can punk off if you came here to flatter me.
That's not why I work—you think I whittle sentences
down to the truest words possible so somebody who
talks like he's constipated will admire me? There's a
café called the Rotonde up the street. You'll get your
money's worth of advice there. Advice from artists is
the cheapest thing on the menu.

When you get this strident, it really saddens me. It
doesn't seem like the real you—at least, not the you I
hear when I read your work. You can't convince me that
someone who writes a sentence as beautiful as this one is
as hardboiled as you pretend to be: "When I saw my wife

again standing by the tracks as the train came in by the piled logs at the station, I wish I had died before I ever loved anyone but her." When you go all bellicose it just seems ... insincere. It makes your admirers wonder what happened to you.

Oh, nerts. You're going to be like all the rest, aren't you? You're going to tell me how much I've influenced you, and then you're going to turn around and tell me all the ways I've failed you. You'll knock me for being famous, say my women characters are flat and unrealistic male fantasies, and then tell me my style was so original I ended up parodying myself. Then you'll let me know exactly when my train went off its tracks. Go ahead. You won't be the first.

You're very defensive, as you usually were with the press and public. Why is that?

Listen, I come from a time when the writing was
supposed to be more important than the writer.
That was the idea behind the movement I was part of.
In modernism you take yourself out of the work so
the reader experiences your words, not you. Writing's
supposed to be about the art, but most readers only
care about personality.

*Aren't you a bit to blame for that? Your fiction is
so transparently autobiographical that readers are
naturally intrigued by the life that inspired it.*

The only writing that's any good is what you make
up, out of your imagination. That's what makes
things ring true. Good writing has truths that aren't
necessarily facts. You do understand the difference
between truths and facts, don't you? Maybe if you
did, you wouldn't accuse me of going phony.

You've certainly had to deal with plenty of half-truths. Is there one particular misperception that irritated you?

Definitely the war. Here's the gen. Papa went to war and got blown up on the Italian front. A few years later Papa went to write about getting blown up, only for dramatic purposes he made his people soldiers instead of ambulance drivers. Papa never claimed to be a soldier, but the newspapers decided he must've been to write so swell about war. That thing you gentlemen just tossed out with baby and bath water both? It's called dramatic license.

It's not that simple, is it? I mean, please don't punch me—but biographers have shown how when you came home from the war you told different versions of what happened to you there. Sometimes you boasted that you carried another man on your back, sometimes that

you bravely told doctors to tend to other wounded first.
Once you claimed you threw away your revolver so you
wouldn't be tempted to shoot yourself.

That mortar didn't care whether I was a combatant
or a canteen boy when it came at me. I've got 227
scars to prove it. As for all that other stuff … okay,
so I gilded a little lily at first. But I never fudged facts
after I became a writer.

Did you try to correct some of those legends that sprouted
up around you?

I spent *years* clearing up the biographical hooey when
I should've been writing. When *The Sun Also Rises*
came out, my publisher ruined a portrait of me by
John Blomshield by trying to fertilize said portrait
with a load of biographical horseshit. The portrait

was very fine but the horseshit stank. Not only did they say I was in the Italian infantry—they said I was a football star and that I fought my way through college as a boxing instructor. Not only was I never a boxing instructor, Christ knows I never went to college!

Maybe it was my fault. I didn't give Scribner's any facts my first time out, so they had to work with what they'd *heard* about me. I was naïve in thinking biography was as unimportant to readers as it was to me. Hell, the same thing happened when they made the first movie version of *A Farewell to Arms* in '32. The Hollywood flacks put out so much horseshit about me, it's a wonder the horse didn't die of dysentery. I had to issue a press release: "Mr. H. appreciates the publicity attempt to build him into a glamorous personality like Floyd Gibbons or Tom Mix's horse Tony but he deprecates it and asks the motion picture people to leave his private life alone."

Clearly, you don't like biography. Why not?

Nothing kills the fiction faster than psychoanalyzing the writer. It's invasive and destructive. It's like in the early '50s, when all the professewers came after me. They were a nightmare combination of junior-G men, Rorschach testers from the Herr Sigmund school, and Kremlin keyhole-peepers. Most weren't professing—they were pursuing.

Things haven't changed much, then. It seems that with every new biography there's a new angle on the very thing you say readers are too fixated on—your personality.

Biographing besieges a guy—it's invasive and inhibiting. *You* try putting new words to paper when you've got a school of interpretation out there saying everything you write about can be traced back to your taking shrapnel in your Balzac in a war. *You* try it when you've got bastards saying you wasted your talent proving your manhood because your mother dressed you like your sister when you were a baby. *You* do that when everybody you ever drank or shot pheasant or baited tackle with has written a memoir diagnosing your neuroses …

So how would you respond to people like Gertrude Stein, who said readers would discover a very different Hemingway if you ever exposed your real self?

I'd borrow a line from "Hills Like White Elephants" and say, "Would you please *please please please please please please* stop talking?" Papa is many people, just like you are many people, dear reader, and personality is a hell of a dull talk. What's important is the work.

If I promise not to psychoanalyze and stick to the
writing, may I join you?

All right. Pull up a chair and order a *distingue* and
cervelas with a plate of *pommes à l'huile*. By the time
they get here you'll have an opening line for your war
story—if you're serious about writing.

While you're making yourself comfortable, I'm
going to give you a nickname. I love nicknames—I
give one to everybody who comes my way. If I don't
think I like you I'll call you something belittling.
And if I don't *dislike* you, I'll call you something
that's only *affectionately* belittling, just so you
remember who's Papa. From here on out, you'll
answer to Maestro, and we'll decide at the end
of these interviews just which of those categories
you fall into.

ON WAR

Hemingway was one of the first writers to depict the dehumanizing psychological effects of combat. Yet war was more than simply his initiation into brutality. In a 1942 anthology he edited, *Men at War*, he described how diametrically opposite the arts of soldiering and writing really are. Whereas the former requires one to live in the moment "with no before and no after," the latter requires suspending disbelief—an imaginative faculty that can get a man killed on the battlefield. Ultimately, Hemingway's interest in war exposes his anxieties about the role of imagination in writing and the place of fiction in everyday life.

Okay, so the story I want to write is about a war that's been going on so long people are inured to it. The casualty count goes up every day, but the home front has tuned it out. They're more concerned with celebrity gossip.

Stop right there. Your story's already been written. It's called "In Another Country." I wrote it in 1927, and you won't top it. You might think you can knock me out of the ring, but you won't. I KO'd all the war-story boys with "In Another Country." Crane?—right hook. Stendhal?—left. Tolstoy?—uppercut.

Oh, yes. I know what you mean—"In Another Country" may be the most underappreciated of your masterpieces. That opening sentence! "In the fall the war was always there, but we did not go to it any more." Fitzgerald said it was one of the most beautiful prose sentences he'd ever read. That's what I love about that story, and other ones

with Nick Adams, such as "Now I Lay Me" and "A Way
You'll Never Be." There's a cathartic fragility in them.
It's typical of the crushing vulnerability of your best
work. You're right—I won't top it.

No, and you won't even get into the fight if you keep
lungeing at me with that many syllables. Cathartic
fragility? Crushing vulnerability? Cripes. Maybe
I should have nicknamed you Faulkner instead of
Maestro. Lay off the adjectives, will you?

Let's say I was heading to war. What would it teach me
about writing?

War's such a great experience for a writer because, as
I once wrote, "it groups the maximum of material and
speeds up the action and brings out all sorts of stuff
that you normally have to wait a lifetime to get."

What "stuff"?

You know what, I may just have to shorten your nickname from Maestro to Mice—you seem a little mousy to me. The meaning's right there for you. Read *In Our Time*. Not all of its vignettes are war scenes, but many are, and each captures a little sliver of experience in a way that's intense and immediate. Among others, you have a kitchen corporal accompanying a battery to Champagne, a soldier "potting" Germans as they come over a garden wall in Mons, the contrast between another soldier's fear while under bombardment and his unwillingness to admit that terror the next night while romping with a whore.

I called these fragments "unwritten stories," because in them there's only a minimum of context— no sense of what has happened or what will come,

only that second of experience in its purity. You don't
need the before or after because the present's all
there—crystalline and transparent, but not, as the
college boys like to think, shallow.

*I see the "unwritten" quality in your stories because
they're so compact. What about your novels, though?
Doesn't a full-length plot demand some before and
after? How did you balance the visceral immediacy
of war against the need to advance the action in*
A Farewell to Arms *or* For Whom the Bell Tolls?

It wasn't easy. It took me ten years after I was blown
up to do *Arms*. I tried a couple of times before
that. Around the time I married Hash—that's what
I used to call Hadley, my first wife—I was trying
to make something out of the war, but I couldn't
find the structure. I thought about jumbling some

fragments together like Scott Fitzgerald did in *This Side of Paradise* but, thank Christ, Mrs. Hemingstein (Hemingstein being a nickname I gave myself as kid) talked me out of that. She did, and so did Gertrude— Miss Stein told me there was too much description and it was lousy to boot and that I should start over. So I did.

One of your main legacies is the psychological duress of combat that you depict in stories like "In Another Country," "Now I Lay Me," and "A Way You'll Never Be." People today take post-traumatic stress disorder for granted, but in the 1920s the concept of "shell shock" was new.

Even though those stories were invented, I knew that stress personally. "In Another Country" was me recuperating in Milan in 1918 with my knee all shot

to strudel with a medal I wasn't sure I deserved, and
unable to sleep. Did I really lie, as I wrote, "in bed
by myself at night, afraid to die and wondering how
I would be when I went back to the front again"?
Of course I did. Maybe not all the time. There were
happy things in Milan, like me and Agnes von
Kurowsky, who became the nurse in *A Farewell to
Arms*—but those weren't important to that story.

"Now I Lay Me" was about going back to the war,
which I never did but I could have, you see, and it
was how I knew I *would've* felt because I was already
feeling that way. By '27, when I was writing both those
stories, I really had "been living for a long time with
the knowledge that if I ever shut my eyes in the dark
and let myself go, my soul would go out of my body,"
as I wrote in "Now I Lay Me." I'd been that way for a
long time ever since I'd been blown up at night and
felt it go out of me and go off and then come back.

So, you see, you have to write about what you know, not what you've studied, and if you haven't seen the bloat of the dead with their pockets pulled out and gone through and all the paper that rains down after a shelling—there's always as much paper as rubble—you've got no business writing about it.

From the look of you, I doubt you've been anywhere near a war. Maybe you should try the Dingo instead of the Rotonde. That might be more your crowd.

I'll ignore the insinuation and simply point out how brilliantly you also depict survivor's guilt.

I did it best in "Soldier's Home." It's about the guilt of telling people the war stories they want to hear: "Harold Krebs felt the need to talk but no one wanted to hear about it. His town had heard too many atrocity stories to be thrilled by actualities. Krebs found that to be listened to at all he had to lie … A distaste for everything that had happened to him in the war set in because of the lies he had told."

So what is the major theme of your war writing? It seems contradictory. The message of A Farewell to Arms *is almost diametrically opposed to that of* For Whom the Bell Tolls. *The first says war is inhumane, but the second says we can find our humanity through it.*

There are many themes in my war work, because war never means just one thing. *In Our Time* was existential before existential existed. In one vignette Nick Adams tells a fellow wounded soldier named Rinaldi that if they can survive they'll each have made their own peace. That was my way of saying that the so-called Great War left those of us who'd been there looking for some individual beachhead of dignity amid the killing fields of existence.

Arms was grimmer. At college they'll teach you to classify it as naturalism. I was saying that what war can't break in you, life will. That's why at the end Catherine and her baby die in childbirth. If they didn't, none of the death that Frederic Henry sees in battle would mean anything—he'd think he could escape it. As I wrote in *Death in the Afternoon*, "All stories, if continued far enough, end in death, and he is no true storyteller who would keep that from you."

For Whom the Bell Tolls was different because that was a different war. I was saying there's real conviction to be had even when what you believe in is being corrupted. Robert Jordan recognizes that and accepts his death. Even if his side will lose the Spanish Civil War, even if the Communists backing his side are as murderous as the Fascists they're fighting, his death is not a waste because he's done his duty with integrity. He's upheld his ideals.

It's worth pointing out how influential your war fiction was outside of literary circles. Generals and grunts alike read you. Politicians, too. It's hard to imagine today's policymakers looking to novels and stories for moral insights into combat.

You're right, but literature back then had real consequences. It wasn't just something to dissertate on. You know who used *For Whom the Bell Tolls* as a manual on guerilla warfare? None other than Fidel Castro. That book was all the formal training he had for overthrowing Batista in Cuba in 1959. Of course, I might've been more flattered if his coup hadn't cost me my favorite house, not to mention a country I loved. *Viva la revolución*, indeed!

ON EXPATRIATION

The success of *The Sun Also Rises* in 1926 helped popularize the phenomenon of expatriation, inspiring young Americans to live abroad, whether in Paris, on the Riviera, in Italy, or in Spain. A 1928 *Harper's* essay, "Babes in the Bois," speaks of the novel's influence on the postwar generation: "Youngsters learned it by heart and … immediately took ship for Paris to be the disciples of the new faith of disaffection …" Hemingway resented his reputation as spokesman for "The Lost Generation," even though *The Sun Also Rises* popularized that term. As he always insisted, some may have gone to Paris for the drink and debauchery, but he went to *work*.

*It's amazing to see the difference between your juvenilia
and what you accomplished shortly after arriving in
Paris in December 1921. What does expatriation teach
a writer?*

It teaches you dislocation, which sharpens the
memory and makes you able to recall details you
take for granted when you're in the actual place
you're writing about. In *A Moveable Feast* I called it
"transplanting yourself," and I said it's "as necessary
with people as with other sorts of growing things."
Here's a little secret: if you want to judge my best
stuff, look for things that aren't set where I was when
I wrote them.

*Like your Michigan stories? If I tried to write something
like "Big Two-Hearted River," I think I'd need to be
in the Upper Peninsula, walking through the burnt-*

timber hills, watching the river water rush the bridge
spiles, touching the grasshoppers that have turned
black to blend in with the devastated environment.
I'd need to be there to make sure I didn't get those
details wrong.

Then you have no imagination. I couldn't have gotten
the country in "River" and "Indian Camp" and "The
End of Something" right if I'd been in Michigan
because I'd only be recording them. By being far away
I could picture those details like an impressionist
painter, like Cézanne. I could give the pine scrub and
heather a dreamy quality, a holy aura that's realer
than real. Now take something that I didn't do from
a ways away—*To Have and Have Not*. That's my Key
West book, and it's not as good as it should've been
because I was in the Keys when I did it. I didn't have
enough distance.

But that's not true for The Sun Also Rises, *is it? Part of its appeal is that it feels like it's being written as its actual events unfold. Much of its attraction is that it's a roman-à-clef, a true-life novel whose names have been changed to protect the guilty.*

The roman-à-clef controversy was a roman-à-crock. All reviewers could talk about was how the real Robert Cohn, Brett Ashley, and Mike Campbell were after me for exposing them as rummies and fornicators. By the way, I'll save you having to look up their real names, ladies and gentlemen—they were Harold Loeb, Duff Twysden, and Pat Guthrie.

Yes, but didn't you once start a sequel in which your dramatis personae confront your narrator? Brett tells Jake Barnes about how tedious it is for her to be cornered in bars by tourists who congratulate her for starring in a

notorious novel. Obviously, the line between fiction and
fact was thin for you, too.

There you go again, discrediting the imagination. *The Sun* has a lot more invented stuff than readers admit. It was important for reviewers to say I just transcribed how expatriates were *tromper*-ing each other because they wanted to believe I was celebrating young people going to pot. I wasn't. I wasn't encouraging anybody to come to Europe to get stewed. I was showing how my generation lacked rituals for making sense of the world.

Regardless, The Sun *made living abroad a fad. To this day, people carry it around Paris and Pamplona, searching for the same bars and restaurants. In a weird way many of them, college students especially, re-enact the book.*

Yes, well, I haven't heard of too many students mangling their cocks in homage to Jake Barnes, who can't love Brett because the war took away his genital abilities. That must mean students have some sense of when to throw the brake, huh? If they think *The Sun* glamorizes expatriate life they should look up stuff that's more straightforwardly critical of wastrels. I did an essay a few months after I came to France, "American Bohemians in Paris." "The scum of Greenwich Village, New York, has been skimmed off and deposited in large ladlesful on that section of Paris adjacent to the Café Rotonde." If that's not clear, get a seeing-eye dog.

Yes, we forget that many Americans in Paris worked, especially the artists. It was the place to meet the modernist literati, whom you quickly became one of.

I wasn't the careerist Miss Stein later made me out to be. While I was lucky to be in the right place at the right time, I never felt like I was part of a movement, not even when my stories started appearing in *The Little Review*, *the transatlantic review*, *This Quarter*, and other "little magazines" that expatriates all over Paris were starting. These were fly-by-night operations. They had a readership of maybe five, but they were five important readers who could make your name. Edmund Wilson was one—he reviewed my first two books, *Three Stories and Ten Poems* and *in our time*, when they had a combined circulation of 480 copies. But I never would've been successful if I hadn't had the goods. And it was in Paris that I got them. You know how, Mice? Hard work.

That brings us to another important topic …

THE HEMINGWAY STYLE

As early as 1927 critics hailed Hemingway as the most influential prose stylist of the era, his descriptive exactitude and taut rhythms making it impossible not to regard the genteel garrulity of Victorian writing as artificial and evasive. "Infectious" was another common description, for no sooner were dialogue, landscape description, and precise word choice identified as his trademark techniques than other writers began imitating them. Hemingway is so frequently parodied that today we forget just how experimental his style was. His patented techniques—most notably, his use of omission—introduced a new dramatic intensity into fiction.

Your literary generation insisted that a writer's goal was to invent novel forms of expression. "Make it new!" Ezra Pound insisted, and, suddenly, how a story was told became more important than what the story was about. How did you discover your style?

I did it the way I describe myself doing it in *A Moveable Feast*—one sentence at a time. When I first came to Paris I rented a room on the rue Descartes and wrote the six truest sentences I could: "If I started to write elaborately, or presenting something, I found that I could cut the scrollwork or ornament out and throw it away and start with the first true simple declarative sentence I had written." Once I did that, I realized that what you don't say says more than what you do. It was a short hop from that to my theory of omission, also known as my "iceberg principle."

Can you remember the story in which you first used omission?

"Out of Season." I wrote it in 1923. Hadley and I were in Cortina, Italy. It was a literal transcription of an argument we had except that, as I later wrote in *Feast*, I "omitted the real end of it which was that the old man"—Peduzzi—"hanged himself."

You know, I consider myself a pretty good reader, but "Out of Season" never made me think of suicide. To me it's always been about marriage.

That's why you don't read by theories, Mice. When I compared the effect of omission to an ice floe—"The dignity of movement of an iceberg is due to only one-eighth of it being above water"—I didn't intend for readers to go diving for that other seven-eighths.

I was only saying that what's below the surface is still there even if you can't see it. The missing part may not be all that relevant. It wasn't in "Season" and I'm not so sure it was in "Big Two-Hearted River," although some professnorers have built careers trying to prove I wasn't joking when I said it was about coming back from the war only the war wasn't in it. Later I got so bored with them asking questions that I sent them chasing a red herring. I said that there were Indians in the story too ... and none of them appeared. That was a joke. Reading isn't meant to be a guessing game.

I don't disagree in the case of "Out of Season," but in something like "Hills Like White Elephants" where the main conflict is only alluded to, isn't it the mystery of what's not explicit that engages the reader? In other words, isn't the interpretive task to figure out what

you've omitted, if only for a basic understanding of
what's going on?

Absolutely not. Crithacks want to classify "Hills
Like White Elephants" as an abortion story because
the word is never used. To classify it that way is
to *crass*ify it. It reduces drama to subject-matter.
The real interest in "Hills" is how the girl, Jig,
and the American pressuring her to undergo the
abortion talk to each other. Their back and forth is
more important than what's making them go back
and forth. It's a story about how men and women
communicate—or how they don't communicate,
that is, because they communicate so differently.

Okay, I can see that, but isn't the subject matter
somewhat important? I mean, there seems to be a lot
of fetal symbolism in the description of the landscape.

Using a simile in the title seems a pretty blatant way of directing readers to it. They're led to wonder what exactly the hills of Spain's Ebro valley have to do with white elephants, and once they make the abortion connection, they associate the hills with Jig's unplanned pregnancy.

Here's a secret for you—All the symbolism that people talk about is shit. I used to get letters from students, *Dear Dr. Hemingstein, My English teacher says the sea in your book about it and that old man is really amniotic fluid. Could you confirm or deny?* ... *Dear Comrade Hemingrrhoid, My professlurer says that Jake Barnes's cock is defective and that this means moral eunuchs rule the world. Is that true?* As I told George Plimpton, it's very bad for a writer to talk about how he writes. He writes to be read by the eye and no explanations or dissertations should be necessary. You can be sure that there's much more than will be read at any first reading and having made this it's not the writer's province to explain it or run guided tours through the more difficult country of his work. So if you want to believe the hills are alive with the sound of babies, you go right ahead. Just leave me out of it.

Is there any other aspect of your writing besides symbolism that you thought critics overemphasized?

Dialogue. Around the time of *Men Without Women* the angleworms decided it was the only thing I was good at. They forgot about landscape, people, and so on and so on. *Vanity Fair* started it in 1928 with an unfunny piece about me using dialogue in the bullring instead of a cape. After that, you couldn't find a parodist that didn't make hay out of it.

Is there a technique or device you used that you feel critics have neglected?

Stream of consciousness. I didn't invent it, of course. James Joyce didn't either, but he made it famous. The lit boys read "Hills" and "The Killers" and other stories, and they thought, "Here's a son of a bitch who won't go into people's heads. He sticks to the outside, like a camera." They ignored how often I went inside.

I do it in the fourth chapter of *Green Hills of Africa*, which almost sounds like Faulkner, which is funny given how often I gave the shepherd's crook to Wild Bill Hiccup. I do it, too, at the end of *To Have and Have Not* when Harry Morgan's wife, Marie, has to confront his death—she's my Molly Bloom. And, of course, there are Harry Walden's dying visions of all the things he failed to write about in "The Snows of

Kilimanjaro," and Robert Jordan's meditations on heroism in *For Whom the Bell Tolls*. So I fished the stream of consciousness and docked at the island of interior monologue a lot more than anyone ever recognized.

Speaking of For Whom the Bell Tolls, *you do something very controversial in the dialogue. The vote seems split as to whether it works.*

You're talking about how the guerillas say, "I obscenity in thy milk," and "Go unprintable yourself," right? Well, Spanish is the greatest language for profanity because it's so formal, and I couldn't do justice to the way the real Pilars and Pablos spoke if I let my publisher pepper the page with dashes which is usually what happened when I tried to use blue words. I once took a copy of

A Farewell to Arms and filled in the blanks: "No
chance of <u>fucking</u>. No place for <u>fucking</u>." Not to shock you,
Mr. Micey Mouse, but that's the way soldiers talk.

I don't doubt it. But what gave you the idea in For
Whom *for translating curses that way? The technique
is almost postmodern in the way it slaps back at censors
who were forever trying to ban your work.*

There you go trying to crassify me again ... but
the idea came when I was escorting a pair of
newspaperwomen around Madrid and our chauffeur
swore up a hurricane when we blew a tire. The girls
wanted to know what he was saying. They were both
bugging me big time, but I couldn't figure out how
to translate that talk in English without it losing its
pique. Even if you could translate Spanish profanity,
it wouldn't sound half as poetic. So I told the

newspaperwomen, "He says expletive deleted in the unprintables of the gearshift of the car's mother," and I thought, "Voilà! That'll be a funny poke to all the censorship slobs." A lot of critics since then have guffawed at it. Even my wife at the time, Martha Gellhorn, thought it was silly.

To me it's more effective than if you'd used the actual words. But that brings us to your reputation as a "dirty" writer. People today forget how much of your early notoriety had to do with your hells, goddamns, *and* sons of bitches. *And those are just the ones you didn't have to replace with a dash.*

The bastards never forgave me for believing a well-placed *fuck* is better than a mealy-mouthed *copulation*. It was bad enough when twits claimed I was a dirt hauler because I wrote about drinking and promiscuity. As late as the mid-'50s turd wrappers like *True* magazine were saying I "took obscene words off the backhouse wall and put them in print." This was after 30 years of my people having their mouths washed out with dashes. You know how silly suppression is? It was okay to say *muck this*, *muck that* but I couldn't say *c—s—r* because the word *cocksucker* would leap too readily into the fine minds of upstanding readers. Well, muck those futhermuckers. Muck the sockcuckers, too. It wasn't until 1937 that I got a single *fuck* into print. That was in *To Have and Have Not*. What nobody understood was that I never used obscenity for gratuitous shock. One should never use words which shock out of all proportion to their own value or connotation, I insisted, but nobody listened.

FICTION vs. NONFICTION

By the mid-1930s, Hemingway's reputation was in free fall thanks to his having abandoned the novel for nonfiction in *Death in the Afternoon* and *Green Hills of Africa*. Critics disparaged this shift, forgetting that Hemingway had begun his career as a journalist and that nonfiction, like war, was his way of keeping his writing grounded in the real world.

What can writing journalism teach me?

It can teach you to avoid all the things that hamstrung Gertie S., Faulkner, Scott F., and Thomas Wolfe—mystification, maundering, and mooning. It can teach you to write a simple declarative sentence. But you have to get out of it fast.

Why?

Because journalism is a racket. It puts a dollar value on your words that's destructive. You're writing to put food on the table, not art for art's sake. I never could've done the *In Our Time* stories if I hadn't quit the *Toronto Daily Star* in 1923.

If that's the case, why did you take journalism up again in the 1930s? You covered the Spanish Civil War for the

North American Newspaper Alliance in 1937–38, and
you were the correspondent for Collier's *during D-Day*
and the liberation of Paris in 1944.

I went back to news because it was the only way of
getting close to those wars. Governments don't see
much purpose in sending an artist to battle, but tell
them you're a journalist, and they'll drive you to the
front in a limousine.

Most of your Toronto pieces from 1920–24 are feature
writing, which is generally considered "soft" news.
Critics have suggested that you were far better suited
to this than the "hard" news of war reporting. They've
been especially hard on your Spanish Civil War
journalism, claiming you were "playing at war" and
that you weren't objective because your anti-Fascism
led you to ignore Communist atrocities. That's all

from a book called The First Casualty *by Philip Knightley, which is taught in introductory journalism classes.*

Maybe Mr. Knighty-Knightley should go back to college himself. I was paid to go to Spain to write about myself going to Spain. Newspapers wanted my take on the situation, and that's what they got. They paid me as much as $1,000 a story when most reporters were getting $25.

Your dispatches from Spain led directly to For Whom the Bell Tolls. *In retrospect, do you think if you'd fictionalized* Death in the Afternoon *and* Green Hills of Africa, *they would have been better received? Many say that such stories as "The Undefeated" and "The Snows of Kilimanjaro" cover the same material but in a more compelling way.*

I did nonfiction books because I had ideas I wanted to talk about, and if you write a novel of ideas, then the fiction goes to pot. I learned that from Tolstoy— I wrote that *"War and Peace* taught me to avoid 'big Political Thought passages,' which aren't as 'true and important and lasting' as the people." If you want to write fiction you have to show ideas through gestures rather than abstractions. But sometimes you want to think Big Thoughts, and that's what nonfiction's for.

What Big Thoughts were you interested in?

How to write. That simple. Even though *Death* and *Green Hills* are about bullfighting and hunting, they're really about writing. I talk about what books are worth reading, why writers should avoid politics, and the elements of a good style. In *Death* I introduced my iceberg principle and in *Green Hills*

I defined the fourth and fifth dimension that prose writing should aim for. Those are concepts, and you can't get conceptual in fiction.

There's something else, too. I wanted to question whether nonfiction is all that different from fiction. There's fiction in both books, after all. I slipped an entire story, "A Natural History of the Dead," into *Death*, as well as an imaginary conversation with a reader who loathes bullfighting. In *Green Hills* I said my purpose was to write an absolutely true book, but then I used fictitious names and novelistic techniques like stream of consciousness. Years later when I did *A Moveable Feast* I said, "If the reader prefers, this book may be regarded as fiction." The same holds for *Death* and *Green Hills*. There are always elements of fiction in nonfiction and if your fiction is any good it'll have the ring of nonfiction, so—why must we label our literature, gentlemen?

ON FOOD, SPORT, AND RITUAL

Hemingway frequently wrote about outdoor endeavors such as hunting, fishing, and, most famously, bullfighting. His works also describe countless meals—some exotic, some as plain as an onion sandwich, yet all depicted with ceremonial lavish. While detractors have been confounded by such seemingly minor fascinations, food and sport are integral to Hemingway's theme of moral engagement, for they are the rituals by which his heroes test their self-control in a world that encourages indulgence. At a time when values were growing increasingly relative, Hemingway viewed how one eats and plays as indices of the strength of character needed to steer clear of temptation.

You've said that writing is like eating—that it's "not conscience, just peristaltic action." That's an unusual metaphor for writing. Can you explain it?

I used that term because peristalsis is the muscular process that's central to digesting. The key word is *process*. Pick any of the things I wrote about and what you'll find is an outline of their process.

Can you give me an example?

Choose any you'd like—eating, fishing, bullfighting, hunting, yencing* ... well, no, I never got that specific with the yencing.

It's easiest to see in bullfighting because appreciating it requires a technical understanding of its traditions. In *Death in the Afternoon* I called

* Yencing is EH's preferred term for copulation.

the process the "certain definite action." Living is
the act of sussing out rules by testing them, so it's
only natural that I wrote about processing experience
by describing the specific steps for surviving
heroically. From the minute I saw my first *corrida*
in 1923 I recognized that bullfighting is an ethical
contest between man and death and that its rules of
engagement provide a graceful, aesthetic analogy to
confronting the violence of being.

Now there are matador characters who meet this
challenge and others who cheat it—Juan Belmonte
in *The Sun*, for example. Belmonte lost his sense of
reality by demanding too many safeguards, and the
crowd knew he was faking. Nino de la Palma was
another. He inspired Pedro Romero, but I no sooner
wrote *The Sun* than Nino was gored and went phooey
with fear. I described his nerved-up performances
in *Death* as "the brave actions of a coward."

Curiously, you write as often about the ethics of
watching the bullfight as of performing it.

There's a right way to follow it, too. In *The Sun* I called
this *afición*—"passion." When you're passionate about
bullfighting, you're not concerned with spectacle but
with expertise—you understand the knowledge that
makes it an art form, and you appreciate the training
behind that artistry. An *aficionado* is dedicated to
preserving that expertise. Unfortunately, Jake Barnes
breaks the aficionado code by introducing Pedro
to Brett Ashley, who seduces and corrupts the boy.
Jake loses his standing among the bullfight insiders
thanks to Brett and the other drunken expatriates.

How does the "certain definite action" relate to hunting
and fishing? Confronting mortality doesn't seem as
evident in them.

Come on safari and let me hear you say you don't face death hunting. If you can't, do the next best thing and read "The Short Happy Life of Francis Macomber." That's about a coward earning his *cojones* back after bolting from a charging lion. He's just about to earn them, too, when his bloody wife blows his head off—whether by accident or design is for you to decide.

Even when mor*tali*ty isn't at stake, how people hunt reveals their mor*ali*ty. *Green Hills of Africa* is me learning that. Through the safari, Papa struggles to not be competitive and braggadocious, those very faults the bastards said I never admitted in print. In the end I come out humbled but respectful of the code.

It's in the fishing stuff, too. Read "Big Two-Hearted River," in which Nick Adams fishes to discover his place in nature. The entire trip is a test. Will he reel in his fish without rushing and breaking the line? Will he spoil the dinner his hiking all day has earned him by eating too fast and burning his tongue? Will he remember not to touch the trout he won't keep with a dry hand so they won't die of fungus? As Nick learns, every single action has consequences. That's the moral of my work.

Interestingly, whenever you write about these rituals, you draw analogies to writing. "River" originally ended with Nick meditating on literary ethics, not fishing.

Writing's a ritual, too. You're still learning the "certain definite action." Read *The Garden of Eden*. David's trying to take shelter from his crumbling marriage in the sanctity of a good sentence. Read *A Moveable Feast*—that's me learning the definite action. It's all the same thing, Mice—the bullfight, the hunt, the river, the sentence. These are the things you must master to make it in a world that's out to break you.

ON FEUDS AND RIVALRIES

Although he owed significant debts to Gertrude
Stein, F. Scott Fitzgerald, and many others,
Hemingway bristled at any suggestion that
his writing was shaped anywhere but in the
crucible of his own literary convictions. His
irritation led him to renounce the influence of
mentors and peers, often in violent language,
such as his professed desire in 1924 to run T.S.
Eliot through a meat grinder. *A Moveable Feast*
provided a later opportunity to settle perceived
scores and ridicule Stein's lesbianism,
Fitzgerald's alcoholism, and John Dos Passos's
illegitimate birth. Such hostility has inspired
much speculation about Hemingway's thin skin
and inveterate competitiveness.

When In Our Time *was published, reviewers declared*
you the "offspring" of Sherwood Anderson and Gertrude
Stein. Was that irritating?

It annoyed me because it wasn't true. In 1922 I did
one story, "My Old Man," that sounded like Sherwood,
and suddenly I'm the fruit of his loins. The danger
of having famous friends is that readers hear their
voices in yours. That's why, from the 1930s on, Your
Author preferred a non-literary crowd. It's better
when only one writer is in the room and best when
you're it. Now, name me something besides "My Old
Man" that sounds like old Sherwon't.

Well, there's The Torrents of Spring, *of course, but*
that's a parody done to declare your independence
from him. Do you regret doing such a hatchet job on
Anderson? He introduced you to Gertrude Stein, after all.

I don't recommend devoting a whole book to telling a bastard he's gone dry. I later apologized: "I did *Torrents* because I was righteous, which is the worst thing you can be ... It was cruel and I was a son of a bitch to do it."

The apology was about 35 years late, though, wasn't it? You wrote that in 1959. Anderson had been dead for nearly 20 years.

Being a friend and being honest aren't the same things. Tell a writer he's great when you know he's faking and you're a phony yourself. Shoot straight and you're an ungenerous bastard. Frankly, I'd rather be a bastard. Friends are a dime a dozen, but good writing is rare.

What did you learn from Gertrude Stein?

I learned repetition, rhythm, and landscape. I never denied what she taught me, not even after she came after me in *The Autobiography of Alice B. Toklas*. I took what I needed from her and moved on, though nobody recognized it. As late as 1934 bastards like Wyndham Lewis were still grousing about "the steining of Hemingway." That's not the gen. When I went to Gertrude's I wasn't wined, dined, *or* steined. Her rhythms are centrifugal, but mine are centripetal. If mine were like hers, I'd never have been able to omit things. Read *The Making of Americans* and you'll see that Gertrude couldn't leave anything out—anything, that is, except the truth.

You were also notoriously hard on F. Scott Fitzgerald. You ridiculed him as a sycophant in "The Snows of Kilimanjaro" and in A Moveable Feast *as an irresponsible drunk. You even have him complaining that his penis is too puny to please Zelda. Did you ever feel you'd been too callous?*

Scott and I had a lot in common. We were both Midwesterners revolting against the genteelorrhea of Midwestern values, but neither of us could stomach bohemians. We believed in hard work, love, and discipline, but we had different attitudes about whether they were achievable. Scott idealized failure. That was his inferiority complex, and it made him easy prey.

"A Matter of Measurements" is the *Feast* chapter you're talking about. You see it as ridicule, but really, I was doing Fitz a favor. I was building his confidence. I took him into the can at Michaud's in Paris to inspect his evidence and assure him he was hung proportionately. You've got to believe you've got the biggest prick in the room if you want to be a great writer. A note to the psychoanaliars: *having* the biggest prick is different from *being* the biggest …

Your friend Donald Ogden Stewart—the inspiration for Bill Gordon in The Sun—*once said that the minute you were beholden to somebody, his days in your circle were numbered: "I think it was a psychological fear he had that you might ask something from him. He didn't want to be overdrawn at your bank." Do you think that's accurate?*

Beetle dung. I'll tell you what *I* once said: "The most essential gift for a good writer is a built-in, shockproof, shit detector." Honest criticism you can trust is how you calibrate that apparatus, and that's what good friends give you. I admit my luck in having them. I had Gertrude to tell me that "remarks are not literature" and so I chopped off

the rambling ending of "Big Two-Hearted River."
Scott was there in June 1926 to convince me that the
opening chapter of *The Sun* was full of "elephantine
facetiousness." That's the kind of marble-mouth
word he liked, but he was right, so I lopped off the
first sixteen pages and the book was stronger. Later
there was John Dos Passos telling me to cut the
preachier parts of *Death in the Afternoon*.

This input is valuable, but you also learn that
friends aren't always right, and you have to
know when they've gypped you with bad advice.
Gertrude was wrong about "Up in Michigan" being
inaccrochable—unfit for public viewing. Virtually
everything Scott said when he sent me a nine-page
critique of *A Farewell to Arms* was screwy, so I wrote
"Kiss My Ass" on his letter and filed it away. Old
Dos was rarely right. I still remember him reviewing
The Sun and calling it a "cock and bull story about a

lot of summer tourists getting drunk." This from a bastard who couldn't invent people if his one good eye depended on it.

If you want to know why I broke with friends, it's very simple: after a while, they had nothing more to teach me.

In the end, there were only two literary relationships that you didn't abruptly terminate—Ezra Pound and Maxwell Perkins.

I almost ended it with Ezra before the friendship really began. He was an affected sort and when I first got to Paris I caricatured him for *The Little Review*. If Lewis Galantière hadn't talked me out of publishing that parody, Ez's ire would've had his Van Dyke spontaneously combusting and he wouldn't have published my first little book, *Three Stories and Ten*

Poems. I knew he and Your Author could get along when he asked me to teach him to box. *He* asked *me*, see? Gertrude learned from me, too—she copied my dialogue—but not only couldn't she ask, she couldn't admit, either.

What about Maxwell Perkins? Thanks to you and Fitzgerald he's the most famous editor in literary history, and yet he seems to have served completely different roles for his authors.

Max was the best editor a writer could have because he only offered as many suggestions as you asked for. Because Scott had no confidence, Max was his handmaiden. Because Thomas Wolfe couldn't put a goddamned story together to save his thyroid gland, Max was his midwife. With me all he had to do was be a friend, and he was a damn fine one. He never asked me to change anything I wrote except to remove certain words which were not then publishable … For me he was not an editor.

Keep in mind he didn't always think my stuff was perfect. We disagreed over *A Farewell to Arms*. He never thought the war and love stories came together in the end. He said that after Frederic and Catherine make it to Switzerland, the war's forgotten, and he wanted Catherine's death linked to it. How the Italian retreat from Caporetto can bloody cause a Caesarean section is beyond me, and I lost my temper. I was so embarrassed by the foul things I said that I asked Max to destroy the letter I said them in—which he did. That was Max. He was wrong about the ending, but I was wrong about getting foul with him.

ON WIVES

Hemingway's tangled marital history suggests
that he was an unrepentant womanizer. Such a
reputation does a great disservice both to him
and to his four wives, all of whom were central
influences. Hadley Richardson, Pauline Pfeiffer,
Martha Gellhorn, and Mary Welsh were strong,
talented women in their own right, in many
ways more complex and more interesting than
the fictional heroines they inspired. Ultimately,
the dissolution of each relationship bespeaks
Hemingway's inability to sustain lasting
emotional ties—a failing he both admitted and
lamented when depicting isolated men defeated
by the complexities of love.

You relied heavily on your wives for literary advice.
Would you consider them collaborators?

That's your word, not mine. I never borrowed from
their diaries or letters like Scott did. None of them
added words or phrases in the margins like Alice
did for Gertrude. Mainly they told me when I was
going phony, and they let me work. Being married to
a writer isn't easy. Your wife has to understand that
when you're not working you're feeling lousy. She
can't distract. That was Scott's problem—Zelda was
jealous of Scott's work. He'd start to work and as soon
as he was working well, Zelda would get bored and
take him off to another drunken party. I may have
had four wives, but none of them ever did that to me.

They also have to understand the difference between
fiction and a writer's real feelings. It couldn't have

been easy on your first wife, Hadley, to be pregnant in
1923 and to read stories about young men dreading the
emotional entanglements of marriage and fatherhood.

You're thinking of "Cross Country Snow," in which
Nick tries to convince his friend George he's excited
about being a father, or the cut part of "Big Two-
Hearted River," in which Nick laments all the friends
he lost after he married. I put it more harshly in
"The Three-Day Blow"—"Once a man's married he's
absolutely bitched."

    What people don't understand is that I was
going for the tragedy of this feeling. I wasn't being
anti-woman. I was saying that men want to love
every bit as much as women, but they're afraid of
complications, and love is always complicating. I
said it best in *Green Hills*. Men "do not want to be
lonesome. They are afraid to be alone in their beliefs

and no woman would love any of them enough so that they could kill their lonesomeness in a woman, or pool it with hers, or make something with her that makes the rest of it unimportant." The problem of being a man is how you handle the complications even when you've a bad habit of daydreaming about escaping them. The only thing escaping gets you *is* lonesomeness, and that's no escape.

After your divorce from Hadley, you expressed great sorrow over leaving her for Pauline Pfeiffer, your second wife. That couldn't have been easy for Pauline. More than any of your wives your writing snipes at her. In "The Snows of Kilimanjaro," Harry takes out his self-hatred on his "rich bitch" wife, blaming his corruption on her family's money. It strikes readers as a little ungrateful considering the Pfeiffer family paid $33,000 to send you on the African safari that inspired that story.

Don't forget to mention that's $33,000 in the heart
of the Depression. All the biographers do that, just
to emphasize how lousy of a lout I was to Pauline.
No, it's true, she didn't get her literary due. See,
no matter how much you go on to love in life, you
always remember the first one because she was there
before you were yourself, and you remember all the
possibilities of who you might have become. With
a second love that starts in adultery like mine and
Pauline's did you always feel guilty. First you're a
couple and then you're a couple with an unmarried
friend and suddenly you're a husband, with two
attractive girls around and if you have bad luck you
get to love them both.

You're quoting from A Moveable Feast, *which portrays
Pauline as "unrelentingly" set on stealing you from
Hadley. It's telling that you don't even use Pauline's*

*name in that book—she's the "unmarried young
woman" and the "temporary best friend."*

Parts of *Feast* about Pauline never made it into print.
I said I never worked better nor was I happier than
with her. That was left out because it was a beginning
not an ending and I was saving it for a later memoir
about love, remorse, contrition, and unbelievable
happiness and the story of truly good work and final
sorrow. If you want a taste of that "unbelievable
happiness," read *Green Hills of Africa*. I call Pauline
P.O.M., or "Poor Old Mama," and it's a very full and
happy picture of our love.

*If you were so happy, why did you begin an affair with
Martha Gellhorn in 1936? Friends said you needed a
new love to write your next "big" book. You had to leave
Hadley after* The Sun Also Rises *and have Pauline to do*

A Farewell to Arms, *and now you had to leave Pauline and have Martha to do* For Whom the Bell Tolls.

Real friends don't theorize. I fell for Marty because she was a writer herself, and she lived to travel, and most of all because she was political. I'd gotten fat in Key West, and I needed my vitality back. The best part of Marty wasn't the marriage. It was being in Madrid with her in '37 and '38 during the Spanish Civil War. We had a fine extramarital time at the Hotel Florida, making love and dodging Generalissimo Franco's shells.

If you don't believe I felt bad, read my play, *The Fifth Column*. There's a line in which a whore tells the hero, Philip Rawlings, not to get kinked up with Dorothy Bridges. "I want to make an absolutely colossal mistake," he says. That's how I felt, and that's what I did.

You both made a mistake. The Fifth Column *is*
disturbing for its negative portrait of Dorothy, whom
you describe as a "bored Vassar bitch" and a "lazy"
writer. Folks have wondered why Ms. Gellhorn didn't
leave you on the spot.

The play was my way of pushing her to leave me.
Rawlings and Dorothy *don't* marry, you see. But
Marty never complained about *The Fifth Column.*
She took it as a joke.

Popular perception is that your third marriage didn't
last because of rivalry, that you felt Martha was more
committed to journalism than to you, especially after
1942, when she was reporting full-time on World War II.

For God's sake, don't quote that telegram: ARE YOU
A WAR CORRESPONDENT OR A WIFE IN MY BED?

I regretted it the minute I sent it, knowing I'd spend
eternity with biogassers citing it back at me. The
rivalry wasn't one-sided. Every time Marty put out
a book, she was compared to her Heminghubby.
And Your Author took the blame for that marriage.
Read *Across the River and Into the Trees*. "You lose
women the same way you lose a battalion; by errors
of judgment, orders that are impossible to fill,
and through impossible conditions. And through
brutality."

Your final marriage to Mary Welsh was your longest—
fifteen years, as opposed to thirteen with Pauline and
five each with Hadley and Martha. Yet it doesn't excite
as much interest as the others.

That's because I wasn't publishing much fiction with
Mary. I was writing a lot—*Islands in the Stream*, *The*

Garden of Eden, and the Africa book—but I only put
out two novels, *Across the River and Into the Trees* and
The Old Man and the Sea. Miss Mary wasn't in either
of them, and readers only want to know your wife
when you make her a character.

*For better or worse, her main literary contribution seems
to be the sexual experimentation you explore in* Garden.
*When a portion of that manuscript was published in
1986, people were shocked by the role swapping between
David and Catherine Bourne. It excited some rather
prurient curiosity about yours and Mary's sex life.*

Another example of how biography is buggery. I
wrote an entry in Miss Mary's diary remembering
a time in Torcello, Italy. "Mary has never had one
lesbian impulse but has always wanted to be a boy …
I loved feeling the embrace of Mary which came to

me as something quite new and outside all tribal law. On the night of December 19th we worked out these things and I have never been happier." From the way the hackademics have latched on to that passage, you'd think I'd written *Lady Chatterley's Lover*. You haven't lived until you've seen speculation that on occasion you enjoyed your wife slipping you a digit ...

Well, I think scholars are trying to do you the favor of understanding your obsession with manliness by saying that those erotic experiments make your thinking on sex and gender more complicated than what the macho stereotype suggests.

If you want to understand what happened in my marriages, re-read "In Another Country." It was never about sex. It was always about love and loss. The Italian major tells Nick he must never marry, because he's bitter over his wife dying of pneumonia: "If a man is to lose everything, he should not place himself in a position to lose anything. He should not place himself in a position to lose. He should find things he cannot lose." If I made one mistake with my wives it's that I put myself in a position to lose, but unlike the major, it was a loss of my own making. You see, I never made myself believe I *couldn't* lose Hash and Mama and Marty and Miss Mary. You have to be absolutely convinced you can't live without the one you love, and I never did and I paid the price … so let's move on, can we?

ON FEMALE CHARACTERS

Conventional wisdom insists that realistic females are rare in Hemingway's writing. His typical heroine, detractors complain, is either compliant and submissive or an emasculating harridan. However, accusations of chauvinism are misplaced. In their rush to condemn Hemingway, critics fail to appreciate the nuances of Catherine Barkley in *A Farewell to Arms* or Maria in *For Whom the Bell Tolls*. Recently, defenders have begun to demonstrate how such characters exemplify the same heroic qualities as their male counterparts. Such efforts have gone a long way toward redressing Hemingway's reputation for misogyny.

There's a perception out there that you were better at basing female characters on women you knew instead of inventing them. People point to the difference between, say, the sensitive wife in "Cat in the Rain" (based on Hadley) and Marie Morgan in To Have and Have Not.

My people were never literal translations of women I knew. Readers assume Catherine Barkley was Agnes von Kurowsky, but Ag herself never saw the resemblance. In truth, Catherine was part Ag, part Hadley, with some Pauline, and even a little of Duff Twysden's Britishness left over from Brett in *The Sun*. What's your problem with Marie Morgan, anyway?

Well, she hardly seems a genuine portrait of working-class womanhood. Her husband, Harry, loses his arm, but all Marie can talk about is how sexually stimulating she finds his new "stump." Even for your ardent fans their lovemaking scene is a bit ... embarrassing.

You sound like the idiotlogues that came after me in the 1930s. They only liked proletarian women when they were baring their breasts to feed malnourished men—*Grapes of Wrath* gals, in other words. Who's doing the stereotyping now? Marie's comforting her husband in that scene, you dope. She's assuring Harry he's still a man even though he's maimed.

That's an interesting defense, but how about the perception that your attitude toward women hardened after your divorce from Hadley?

I see where this is going. You're saying, "Listen, Hymenstein, with Brett you showed how a woman goes tragic by expressing her need for love through promiscuity, but then you go create what could have been a similar character with Helène Bradley in *To Have* and all you can do is call her a bitch."

Ignore *To Have and Have Not*—at least the parts that aren't about Harry and Marie. The rest is a botch. Helène Bradley was supposed to show what a damn tragedy it is for a woman to get caught in a loveless marriage, but I couldn't say what I wanted to because I'd based Helène and her husband, Tommy, on Jane and Grant Mason, friends of mine from Cuba, and the portrait was libelous. That's the writer's predicament—you want to show the real sorrow in somebody's situation but you've got to worry about lawsuits. If I hardened after Hadley, it was because I hated lawyers, not women.

Did you ever regret calling your second story collection Men Without Women? *Some see the title as a taunt—it almost challenges people not to view you as anti-female.*

What I regret is how Scribner's advertised the title.
Max Perkins took a line without asking from a letter
in which I said the softening feminine influence
is absent in my stories either through training,
discipline, death, or situation. A lot of women,
Virginia Woolf included, came after me for that.

That's ironic given that Men Without Women's
most famous story is "Hills Like White Elephants,"
*which many consider your most sympathetic portrait
of a woman.*

They say that about Jig because the American who
wants her to have an abortion is so obviously a
crut. That's clear villainy. I happen to think I did
much better women elsewhere—Catherine in *Arms*,
for example. Reviewers complained she was too
romanticized. Hell, even Fitz said that. What they

didn't get was that Catherine was romanticizing *herself*. She's trying to escape the war by assuming the trappings of courtly love. The slightly formal way she talks is supposed to clue you to that. I knew it wasn't real—that was my point. For both Frederic and her, idealizing love is a survival mechanism.

Is that also true for Maria in For Whom the Bell Tolls?

It's very true. The critpricks couldn't believe that a woman so recently gang-raped by fascists could find her way into an American's sleeping bag, but Robert Jordan is Maria's way of overcoming her trauma. Choosing to love is her taking control of her life from the futhermuckers who violated her.

Here's what I don't get, Mice. They knock me for being macho, but when I do a sincere love story, I'm ridiculed. You know, of course, that the most mocked line I ever wrote is from *For Whom*: "Did thee feel the earth move?" That's what Robert Jordan says after he and Maria make love. People assume he wants acknowledgment of what a great lover he is, but really he wants some assurance that their union is spiritual and transcendent. I wanted the lovers' dialogue to sound like metaphysical poetry, which was not inappropriate for a book whose title and epigraph come from John Donne. A spiritual union is all Robert and Maria have to endure war.

Your third most controversial heroine is probably Catherine Bourne in The Garden of Eden. *She seems to pay the price for her unconventional sexuality by going insane. The fact that her husband, David, "cures" Catherine's bisexual lover, Marita, of her lesbian tendencies likewise suggests that the book endorses conventional heterosexual roles.*

I don't endorse or enforce anything. I show people in the thick of what they're going through. Catherine and David have a very adventurous love life at first, but the role reversals scare him. Games are exciting but when a man faces the prospect of losing power permanently in a relationship he's going to revert to simple beliefs, and there's no simpler one than the idea that men are men and women are women. That's the tragedy for David. He can't give up being the man. That's the point, not that he *should* be the man. If there's a problem with how that idea gets conveyed, it's because too much of the story is narrated through David's perspective. There are unpublished parts that let the reader sympathize more with Catherine and Marita, but they didn't make it into the final book. If I'd had the guts to put *Eden* out when I was writing it, nobody would've ever accused me of machismo.

Let's imagine a woman averse to reading you because of your reputation. How would you encourage her to overcome that prejudice?

I'd say, "If you don't like me, dear reader, put your finger over the header where it says BY ERNEST HEMINGWAY and pretend you're reading someone else. You'll hear voices that don't sound a whit like you think I sound." Even better, I'd say pretend you're not reading *anybody*. You'll be surprised, I promise. You'll discover that my Catherines and Marias and Maritas gain dimension and come to life when they're no longer thought of as my creations. The great thing about people is that they can be read in many different and contradictory ways. When you hear them through the lips of the writer, though, you only hear what you think the writer is saying. The truth, as always, is more complicated.

THE PRICE OF FAME

While the 1940s and 50s were years of artistic
decline for Hemingway, they conversely
mark the apex of his fame. Interestingly,
commentators often attribute his downward
spiral to his celebrity as much as to alcoholism
and depression. As one recent reviewer glibly
remarks, "Ernest Hemingway was the first
American celebrity writer, and it probably killed
him." Such assertions imply that Hemingway
could have sustained his art had he simply
avoided the spotlight, a claim that ignores the
audience's non-literary desire to revere and
emulate media heroes.

When were you first aware of your celebrity?

I always had a talent for attracting publicity. I was no sooner off the ship after World War I than the *New York Sun* wanted a dockside interview with the first American wounded in Italy. I was page 8 news there and page 3 in the *Chicago American*—WORST SHOT-UP MAN IN U.S. ON WAY HOME.

Real celebrity didn't start until 1929, though. There was some early press in the *In Our Time* years, but they were about me being a writer and not about me being me. Then suddenly I'm in Paris boxing at the American Club with a journalist named Morley Callaghan with Fitz keeping time on our one-minute rounds. Only Scott is lousy at timekeeping and he lets a round go *four* minutes, at which point Your Author has sustained several shots to the kisser and is going down. Lo and behold, the story makes the papers.

Callaghan KOs Hemingstiff! It was the tone that taught me what celebrity is about—it's about debunking you. The press wants to show that Papa's not the man he says he is if another bastard can draw blood first …

It doesn't take 30 years of that speculation to start wondering if they're right. It happens when you realize you're *acting* like yourself to prove the press wrong. Then, when they still doubt you, you find yourself *exaggerating* who you are, and by then, it's really too late, and you're a damned cartoon.

Why didn't you just change your public image if you felt forced to live up to it?

Do that and you're admitting you've been pulling the wool over the public the entire time. And that's when they really turn on you. Every interview, every photograph, every personality profile had to authenticate your image, even when the facts were cockeyed. "Here, Hem," the press boys would say, "sit next to this dead lion so we can snap one for *Life*—we know you didn't shoot the bugger, but we know you *could* have. So what if it's not the gen?" … "Hey, Hem, let us *Town & Country* saps describe you working in your study. What's that? You're black ass and on the block right now because we're looking over your shoulder? Who cares? Just pretend!" There was only one time I tried to change my image, and it blew up like a trench mortar.

Let me guess—Lillian Ross's 1950 New Yorker *profile. People still argue over whether she was mocking you.*

She wasn't. *I* was mocking me—the legend of me, anyway. I was tossing manure about socking

Dostoevsky and Tolstoy, making up stories, talking punch-drunk, but everybody took it seriously. Readers wanted the "real" Hem, but sometimes I get so damn tired of sounding like me that I invent ways of not sounding like me. Lillian didn't know I was pulling her leg, and the next thing I know the press is calling me a deluded coot.

One thing that profile painfully exposes is your heavy alcohol consumption. There are photos galore of you inebriated in the 1950s. Given the press's emphasis on "boozing," do you ever wish you'd been a bit more discreet about drinking?

My generation grew up drinking behind closed doors. By the time we'd lived through twelve years of Prohibition, we'd earned the right to do it in public. I wouldn't trust a man I couldn't see drunk.

*All I'm saying is that alcohol not only impinged on
your output but negatively affected perceptions of you.
"Boozing" is one of those things that people who've
never read you think they know about you.*

Don't diagnose me! Anybody who says I reveled in
rummyhood hasn't read my books. Drinking's a
discipline—that's what Jake forgets in *The Sun* and it's
why he ruins Pamplona for himself. Maybe I didn't
have that discipline myself but I created people who
tried to gain it. Next subject, please.

*Okay ... Did you ever have second thoughts about
writing for slicks like* Life, Holiday, *and* Look *in the
1950s? Articles such as "The Great Blue River" and "The
Dangerous Summer" seemed to damage your literary
reputation, with critics dismissing them as image
management rather than art.*

The crityaks were jealous. *Life* paid $90,000 for "The Dangerous Summer." I deserved the money after giving so much for so long. These pieces weren't supposed to be part of "the reputation." I was writing for a different audience. Some readers desired the simple, pleasant Papa, and for $90,000 I was happy to give it to them. If those articles aren't up to standards, gentlemen, go seek out *A Moveable Feast* and you'll have the Hemingway you want.

Is there anything final you'd like to say?

Only that if we could have made this enough of a dialogue, it would've had everything in it that matters—everything about the writing, that is. It would have the clicking oarlocks of the canoes in "Indian Camp" and the limestone foundation of the deserted sawmill in "The End of Something" and the whap of the blackjack on Ad Francis's skull in "The Battler." It would have the acetylene flares on the avenue des Gobelins that Jake and Brett notice in *The Sun* and the way Ole Andreson's feet hang over the end of his bed in "The Killers." It would include the ants trying to escape the burning log in *A Farewell to Arms* and the old man's stack of brandy saucers in "A Clean, Well-Lighted Place." It would have the dry smell of heather in *For Whom the Bell Tolls* and the slosh of the shark waters in *The Old Man and the Sea*. It would have the seal skins you attached to the bottom of the skis to climb the funicular-less slopes in Schruns in *A Moveable Feast*, and it would have so much more, too, because there *was* so much more …

It would have every detail that I worked hard to pack into every sentence, and *work*'s the word I want you to walk away with—not personality, not fame, not reputation, not Paris nor Papa nor *Papa dobles* at the Floridita nor a shotgun barrel on a summer Ketchum morning when there was finally peace after so much pain. The only thing that matters is the work. The pleasure of doing it well was the only reason I ever wanted to write, and it's a pleasure I look forward to feeling in the seconds after you leave me when I'll press this pencil to this paper and if I'm lucky I'll have earned the right to smile and say, *Yes, yes, old Hem, you've poured difficult emotions into a fine and durable sentence but now there's the next one to do so don't get too content. There is and always will be work to do.*

Still, there's no greater satisfaction than finishing a good sentence, Mice. Remember that if you remember nothing else.

ACKNOWLEDGMENTS

The publishers wish to thank the following for their permission to reproduce the copyright material in this book. Every effort has been made to trace copyright holders, but if anyone has been omitted we will, if informed, make corrections in any future edition.

For their help in obtaining permissions, the author thanks Lydia Zelaya, Permissions Dept., Simon & Schuster, and James H. Meredith, President, The Ernest Hemingway Society and Foundation (www.hemingwaysociety.org)

NORTH AMERICA

Quotations from *Across the River and Into the Trees*, Copyright 1950 by Ernest Hemingway. Copyright renewed © 1978 by Mary Hemingway. Quotations from Ernest Hemingway in "The Art of Fiction," which originally appeared in *The Paris Review* 55 (Spring 1958), used by permission of Scribner, an imprint of Simon & Schuster Adult Publishing Group, on behalf of the Hemingway Foreign Rights Trust. Quotations from "The Art of the Short Story" by Ernest Hemingway, which originally appeared in *The Paris Review* 79 (1981), copyright 1981 by the Ernest Hemingway Foundation. Used by permission of Scribner, an imprint of Simon & Schuster Adult Publishing Group, on behalf of the Hemingway Foreign Rights Trust. Quotations from *By-Line Ernest Hemingway*, edited by William White. Copyright 1934 by Ernest Hemingway and renewed © 1962 Mary Hemingway and By-Line Ernest Hemingway, Inc. Copyright © 1967 By-Line Ernest Hemingway, Inc. Copyright renewed © 1995 by Patrick Hemingway and John H. Hemingway. Quotations from *Death in the*

imprint of Simon & Schuster Adult Publishing Group. Copyright © Hemingway Foreign Rights Trust. Quotations from "On Writing," in *The Nick Adams Stories* reprinted with permission of Scribner, an imprint of Simon & Schuster Adult Publishing Group. Copyright © 1969 Mary Hemingway. Copyright © 1972 The Ernest Hemingway Foundation.

LIST OF CITATIONS

Note: all works by Ernest Hemingway were first published by Charles Scribner's Sons (New York) unless otherwise stated.

p.13 "He wanted ..." / "He was ..." "On Writing" in *The Nick Adams Stories*, ed. Philip Young (1972), p.238.

p.15 "First there ..." / "Then there ..." *Green Hills of Africa* (1935), p.27.

p.19 "the best rules ..." *Conversations with Ernest Hemingway*, ed. Matthew J. Bruccoli (Jackson: University of Mississippi, 1986), p.21.

p.19 "Use short sentences" / "Avoid ..." Quoted in Charles Fenton, *The Apprenticeship of Ernest Hemingway: The Early Years* (New York: Viking, 1954), p.33.

p.23 "postcards from hell" Quoted in Michael Reynolds, "Hemingway's *In Our Time*" in *Modern Short Story Sequences: Composite Fictions and Fictive Communities*, ed. J. Gerald Kennedy (New York: Cambridge University Press, 1995), p.38.

p.24 "I am inclined ..." Edmund Wilson, review of *in our time*, *Dial* 77 (October 1924), p.340.

pp.28–29 "I was always ..." / "I had seen ..." *A Farewell to Arms* (1929), p.185.

p.31 "a lack of growth" / "monotonous repetition ..." William Troy, review of *Winner Take Nothing*, in *Hemingway: The Critical Heritage*, ed. Jeffrey Meyers (London: Routledge and Kegan Paul, 1982), pp.181–182.

p.32 "big slob" Michael Reynolds, *Hemingway: The 1930s* (New York:

Norton, 1996), pp.104–105

p.40 "I want to ..." / "Not as a man ..." *Ernest Hemingway: Selected Letters*, ed. Carlos Baker (1981), p.712.

p.42 "a disguise ..." Gertrude Stein, quoted in John Hyde Preston, "Conversation," *Atlantic Monthly* 156 (August 1935), p.191.

p.42 "his own worst-drawn character" Edmund Wilson, review of *Green Hills of Africa*, in *Hemingway: The Critical Heritage*, p.218.

pp.43–44 "When I saw ..." *A Moveable Feast* (1964), p.210.

p.48 "Mr. H appreciates ..." *Selected Letters*, p.379.

p.50 "Would you *please* ..." "Hills Like White Elephants" in *The Short Stories of Ernest Hemingway*, p.277.

p.53 "In the fall ..." "In Another Country" in *The Short Stories of Ernest Hemingway*, p.266.

p.54 "it groups ..." *Selected Letters*, p.176.

p.58 "in bed ..." "In Another Country" in *The Short Stories of Ernest Hemingway*, p.270.

p.58 "been living ..." "Now I Lay Me" in *The Short Stories of Ernest Hemingway*, p.363.

pp.59–60 [Harold Krebs] felt ..." "Soldier's Home" in *The Short Stories of Ernest Hemingway*, p.145.

p.61 "All stories ..." *Death in the Afternoon* (1932), p.122.

p.63 "Youngsters learned it ..." Richmond Barret, "Babes in the Bois," quoted in Kirk Curnutt, *Ernest Hemingway and the Expatriate Modernist Movement* (New York: Manly, 2000), pp.133–134.

p.64 "transplanting yourself" / "as necessary ..." *A Moveable Feast*, p.5.

p.68 "The scum of ..." "American Bohemians in Paris" in *By-Line: Ernest Hemingway*, ed. William White (1968), p.21.

p.71 "If I started ..." *A Moveable Feast*, p.12.

p.72 "I omitted ... the old man hanged himself" Ibid., p.75.

p.72 "The dignity of movement ..." *Death in the Afternoon*, p.192.

p.73 coming back from the war only the war wasn't in it. /

there were Indians ... appeared.
"The Art of the Short Story" in
*New Essays on the Short Stories
of Ernest Hemingway*, ed. Jackson
J. Benson (Durham: Duke
University Press, 1990), p.5.

p.75 All the symbolism ... is shit.
Selected Letters, p.780.

**pp.75–76 it is very bad ... country
of his work.** *Conversations*, p.120.

p.76 *Vanity Fair* ... John Riddell,
"A Parody Interview with Mr.
Hemingway" in *Vanity Fair* 29
(January 1928), p.78.

p.79 "No chance ..." A page
from this copy is reprinted in
*The Only Thing that Counts: The
Ernest Hemingway–Maxwell Perkins
Correspondence*, ed. Matthew J.
Bruccoli (Columbia: University of
South Carolina Press, 1996), p.103.

**p.81 took obscene words ...
in print.** Quoted in Reynolds
Hemingway: The Final Years (New
York: Norton, 1999), p.292.

p.81 One should ... connotation
Selected Letters, p.211.

**p.86 *War and Peace* taught me
..."** "Old Newsman Writes" in *By-*

Line: Ernest Hemingway, p.184.

p.87 fourth and fifth dimension
Green Hills of Africa, p.27.

**p.87 to write an absolutely true
book / "If the reader ..."** See,
respectively, the foreword to *Green
Hills* and the preface to *Feast*.

p.89 "not conscience ..."
"On Writing" in *The Nick Adams
Stories*, p.218.

p.90 "certain definite action"
Death in the Afternoon, p.21.

**p.90 nerved-up performances /
"the brave actions ..."** Ibid., p.90

p.96 "I did [*Torrents*] ..." "The
Art of the Short Story," pp.100–101.

p.97 "the steining of Hemingway"
Wyndham Lewis, "The Dumb Ox:
A Study of Ernest Hemingway" in
Hemingway: The Critical Heritage,
p.195.

p.99 "I think it was ..." Donald
Ogden Stewart, "An Interview,"
Fitzgerald–Hemingway Annual
(1973), p.85.

p.99 "The most essential ..."
Conversations, p.109.

p.99 "remarks are not literature"
Gertrude Stein, *The Autobiography of*

Alice B. Toklas (New York: Harcourt, Brace, 1933), p.216.

p.100 "elephantine facetiousness" F. Scott Fitzgerald, *A Life in Letters*, ed. Matthew J. Bruccoli (New York: Scribner's, 1994), p.143.

pp.100–101 "cock and bull …" John Dos Passos, "A Lost Generation" in *John Dos Passos: The Major Nonfiction Prose*, ed. Donald Pizer (Detroit: Wayne State University Press, 1988), p.93.

pp.102–103 He never asked … an editor. *Conversations*, p.118.

p.105 Zelda … drunken party. *A Moveable Feast*, pp.180–181.

p.106 "Once a man's …" "The Three-Day Blow" in *The Short Stories of Ernest Hemingway*, p.122.

pp.106–107 "do not want to be …" *Green Hills of Africa*, p.22.

p.108 with two attractive girls around / if [you] … them both. *A Moveable Feast*, pp.209–210.

p.109 I never worked better nor was I happier / it was a beginning not an ending / love, remorse …

final sorrow. Quoted in Bernice Kert, *The Hemingway Women* (New York: Norton, 1984), pp.484–485.

p.110 "I want to make …" *The Fifth Column* (1938), p.42.

p.111 "bored Vassar bitch" / "lazy" Ibid., p.19.

p.112 "You lose [women] …" *Across the River and Into the Trees* (1950), p.57.

pp.113–114 "Mary has never …" Mary Hemingway, *How It Was* (New York: Knopf, 1976), pp.369–370.

p.115 "If [a man] is …" "In Another Country" in *The Short Stories of Ernest Hemingway*, p.271.

p.120 "the softening …" / "either through …" *Selected Letters*, p.245.

p.122 "Did thee feel …" *For Whom the Bell Tolls*, p.160.

p.125 "Ernest Hemingway was …" L.S. Klepp, review of *True at First Light* by Ernest Hemingway, in *Entertainment Weekly* (July 7, 1999), p.67.

p.129 I get so … like me. Quoted in A.E. Hotchner, *Papa Hemingway* (New York: Random House, 1966), p.117.

REFILL?

BIOGRAPHY
Carlos Baker, *Hemingway: A Life Story* (London: Collins, 1969; New York: Scribner's, 1969)
James R. Mellow, *Hemingway: A Life Without Consequences* (London: Hodder and Stoughton, 1993; Boston: Houghton Mifflin, 1992)
Michael S. Reynolds, *The Young Hemingway* (London: Blackwell, 1986); *Hemingway: The Paris Years* (London: Blackwell, 1989); *Hemingway: The American Homecoming* (London: Blackwell, 1992); *Hemingway: The 1930s* (London: Blackwell, 1996); *Hemingway: The Final Years* (London and New York: Norton, 1999)

CRITICAL STUDIES
Lawrence R. Broer and Gloria N. Holland, *Hemingway and Women: Female Critics and the Female Voice* (Tuscaloosa: University of Alabama Press, 2002)

Scott Donaldson, *The Cambridge Companion to Ernest Hemingway* (London and New York: Cambridge University Press, 1996)
Scott Donaldson, *Hemingway vs. Fitzgerald* (Woodstock: Overlook Press, 1999)
Linda Wagner-Martin, ed., *A Historical Guide to Ernest Hemingway* (London and New York: Oxford University Press, 2000)

TRAVEL AND COFFEE-TABLE BOOKS
Craig Boreth, *The Hemingway Cookbook* (Chicago: Chicago Review Press, 1998)
Michael Palin, *Michael Palin's Hemingway Adventure* (London: Weidenfeld Nicolson Illustrated, 2000; New York: Thomas Dunne, 2000)
Frederick Voss and Michael Reynolds, *Picturing Hemingway: A Writer in his Time* (New Haven: Yale University Press, 1999)

INDEX